This *LADYBIRD TALE*
belongs to

....

Rapunzel

Retold by Vera Southgate M.A., B.COM
with illustrations by Yunhee Park

LADYBIRD 🐞 TALES

ONCE UPON A TIME there lived a man and his wife. They had everything that they wanted in the world, except for one thing.

For many years, they had longed to have a child whom they could love. Yet no baby was born to them.

At the back of their house was a window which looked out over a beautiful garden, full of lovely flowers and fine vegetables.

The garden was surrounded by a high wall. No one ever tried to climb the wall, for the garden belonged to a witch, who was feared by everyone.

One day, the wife stood at the window, looking down into the garden. In one of the vegetable beds, she saw some fresh, green salad. It looked so tempting that she longed to eat some.

Every day that followed, she looked out of the window at the fresh, green salad. The more she looked at it, the more she longed to eat it. Soon she did not want anything else to eat.

She grew pale and thin because she knew she could not have the salad. Her husband grew worried when he saw how thin she had become.

"What is the matter with you, dear wife?" he asked.

His wife pointed to the fresh, green salad in the witch's garden.

"Ah!" she sighed. "If I cannot eat some of that salad, I shall surely die."

"Rather than let you die," replied the man, "I shall climb into the witch's garden and bring you some salad."

The man waited until twilight, then climbed over the high wall into the witch's garden. There he quickly gathered a handful of salad and scrambled back over the wall.

His wife sat down at once and ate the salad. It tasted even better than she had imagined. It tasted so good that, by the next day, she was longing for more salad. So, once more, her husband felt that he must climb over the wall to fetch it for her.

Waiting until twilight again, the man clambered up the wall and lowered himself into the garden. As his feet touched the ground, he nearly fell down with fright, for there stood the witch, in front of him.

"How dare you come into my garden!" she shouted angrily. "And how dare you steal my salad!"

"It was for my wife," replied the poor man. "She longed so much for the salad that, if she could not have had it, she would have pined away and died."

When the witch heard the man's tale, she lost her anger and took pity on him.

"If what you say is true," she said, "I will let you take as much salad as you wish, if you promise me one thing. When your wife has a child, you must give it to me. I shall treat it well and look after it like a mother."

The poor man was so frightened that he agreed. Then he quickly gathered an armful of salad and ran back to his wife.

Some time later, a beautiful baby girl was born to the man and his wife. That very same day, the witch appeared. She reminded the man of his promise, and took the child away with her.

The witch named the baby, Rapunzel. As the child grew, she became the most beautiful girl in the world.

When Rapunzel was twelve years old, the witch shut her up in a tower in the forest. This tower had neither a door nor a staircase but, right at the top, there was one small window.

When the witch came to visit Rapunzel, she stood at the foot of the tower and cried,

"Rapunzel, Rapunzel,
Let down your hair."

Rapunzel had wonderful, long, fine hair, the colour of gold. Whenever she heard the voice of the witch, she threw her long plait of hair out of the window. It was so long that it fell right to the ground.

The witch would catch hold of the hair as if it were a rope. Then she would climb up the wall of the tower and in at the window.

When Rapunzel had been in the tower a few years, it happened that a prince rode through the forest. As he passed by the tower, he heard the sound of someone singing.

The singing was so lovely that the prince stopped to listen. The song came from the top of the tower. It was Rapunzel, singing to herself. The prince wanted to go into the tower to find the singer. He looked for a door but could not find one, so he rode sadly home.

Yet the prince could not forget the sweet song and he longed to see the singer. Every day, he returned to the forest and stood by the tower, listening to Rapunzel singing.

One day, when the prince was standing behind a tree, the witch came to the tower. He heard her say,

"Rapunzel, Rapunzel,
Let down your hair."

Immediately a long thick plait of golden hair fell down to the ground. The prince watched, amazed, as the witch climbed up the tower and in at the window.

The next day, at twilight, the prince stood by the foot of the tower and cried,

"Rapunzel, Rapunzel,
Let down your hair."

Immediately, the plait of hair came tumbling down and the prince climbed up. Rapunzel was surprised, and rather afraid, when she found that a man had climbed up to her room in the tower.

As for the prince, when he saw the beauty of Rapunzel, he was overjoyed. He talked kindly to her and she soon lost her fear. He told her how, for many months, he had stood outside the tower every day, listening to her sweet singing.

So, for many months, the prince visited Rapunzel every evening and they grew to love each other. After a while, the prince asked her to marry him and they talked of how Rapunzel could get out of the tower.

At last Rapunzel thought of a plan.

"Every evening, when you come to see me," she said to the prince, "bring a skein of silk. I shall weave the silk into a ladder. When it is long enough to reach the ground, I shall come down. Then you can carry me away on your horse."

They agreed on this plan. Every night the prince brought a fresh skein of silk, and every day Rapunzel wove a little more of the ladder.

During all this time, the witch knew nothing of the prince's visits to Rapunzel. Then one day, after the witch had climbed up the tower by the plait of hair, Rapunzel spoke without thinking.

"How is it, good mother," she asked, "that you feel so much heavier than the prince?"

"Oh! You wicked child!" cried the witch. "I thought that I had separated you from all the world, but now I find that you have deceived me!"

In her anger, the witch seized a pair of scissors and cut off Rapunzel's beautiful hair. She then took the poor girl away to a desert, and left her weeping. That same night, the witch returned to the tower. The prince arrived and cried,

"Rapunzel, Rapunzel, Let down your hair."

The witch fastened Rapunzel's plait to a hook and threw it out of the window.

The prince climbed up and found himself face to face, not with his beautiful Rapunzel, but with the angry witch.

"Ah!" cried the witch, mocking him. "You have come to find your lady-love. But she is gone and you will never see her again."

The prince thought that Rapunzel was dead. In his sorrow, he jumped from the high window of the tower and fell to the ground. He was not killed but his eyes were scratched by the thorns among which he fell.

For some years the poor, blind prince wandered sadly through the forest. His only food was the roots and berries he found there. He did not care about anything. His only thought was that he had lost his dear Rapunzel.

At last he came to the desert where Rapunzel lived in sorrow. In the distance, he heard her singing and he knew her voice at once.

The blind prince stumbled towards the voice he loved. As soon as she saw him, Rapunzel knew that this poor man in rags was her prince. She ran into his arms.

She was so glad to see him and so sad to find him blind, that her tears fell quickly. Two large teardrops fell upon his eyes. Immediately he could see as well as ever he had done.

How happy Rapunzel and the prince were to be together again! It did not matter to them that they were in rags. They forgot the sad years behind them.

Hand in hand, they made their way happily through the forest to the prince's kingdom. There they were married and lived happily ever after.

A History of
Rapunzel

Its enduring and timeless quality has meant the story of *Rapunzel* has inspired a number of films. She appears as a character in the *Shrek* films and, in 2010, the Disney film, *Tangled*, retold this well-loved fairy tale once more.

Many versions of *Rapunzel* have been told throughout Europe and America over the centuries. The best-known version of this story appeared in *Children's and Household Tales* by the Brothers Grimm, in 1812. The brothers based their version on a 1697 tale, *Persinette*, by Charlotte-Rose de Caumont de La Force. Another influence was the story *Petrosinella*, written by Giambattista Basile for his 1634 collection of tales.

The story of *Rapunzel* has evolved over the years, but the theme of a young woman imprisoned in a tower by a witch has always remained.

Vera Southgate's 1968 retelling is a classic of its time and this new edition of her well-loved version will help to bring the story to a new generation.

Collect more fantastic
LADYBIRD 🐞 TALES

9781409311126

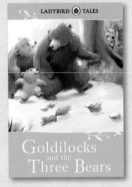

9781409311119

9781409311072

9781409311102

9781409311096

9781409311089

9781409311065

9781409311133

Puss in Boots

9781409311225

Rapunzel

9781409311195

Rumpelstiltskin

9781409311164

The Elves and the Shoemaker

9781409311188

Snow White and the Seven Dwarfs

9781409311171

The Enormous Turnip

9781409311218

The Magic Porridge Pot

9781409311201

Sleeping Beauty

9781409311157

Endpapers taken from series 606d,
first published in 1964

A catalogue record for this book is available from the British Library

Published by Ladybird Books Ltd
80 Strand London WC2R 0RL
A Penguin Company

005

© Ladybird Books Ltd MMXII

LADYBIRD and the device of a Ladybird are trademarks of Ladybird Books Ltd

ISBN: 978-1-40931-119-5

Printed in China